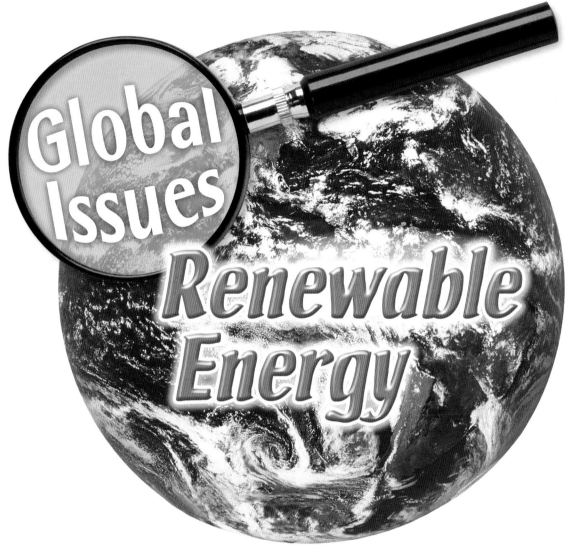

Global Issues

Renewable Energy

Cheryl Jakab

MACMILLAN
LIBRARY

First published in 2009 by
MACMILLAN EDUCATION AUSTRALIA PTY LTD
15–19 Claremont Street, South Yarra 3141

Visit our website at www.macmillan.com.au or go directly to www.macmillanlibrary.com.au

Associated companies and representatives throughout the world.

National Library of Australia
Cataloguing-in-Publication data

Jakab, Cheryl.
    Renewable energy / Cheryl Jakab.
    ISBN: 9781420267402 (hbk.)
    Series: Jakab, Cheryl. Global issues.
    Includes index.
    For primary school students.
    Subjects: Renewable energy sources - Textbooks.
333.794

Edited by Julia Carlomagno
Text and cover design by Cristina Neri, Canary Graphic Design
Page layout by Christine Deering and Domenic Lauricella
Photo research by Jes Senbergs

Printed in China

Acknowledgements
The author and the publisher are grateful to the following for permission to reproduce
copyright material:

Front cover photograph: Solar panels, © Eliza Snow/Istockphoto

Photos courtesy of: AFP Photo/Fred Dufour/AAP, 7 (top), 17; AP Photo/AAP, 24; AP Photo/Rodney
White/AAP, 19; East Japan Railway Company (JR East), 23; AFP/Getty Images, 26, 13, 7 (bottom
right); Getty Images, 29; © Rob Broek/Istockphoto, 15; © Hywit Dimyadi/Istockphoto, 5; © Peter
Eckhardt/Istockphoto, 14; © eliandric/Istockphoto, 10 © Valerie Koch/Istockphoto, 20; © Leif
Norman/Istockphoto, 12; © Hugo de Wolf/Istockphoto, 27 © Jeffrey Zavitski/Istockphoto, 28; Courtesy
of Pelamis, 11; Photolibrary, 7 (bottom left), 9 Photolibrary/ © Ricardo Beliel/Brazil Photos/Alamy, 6
(bottom), 25; Photolibrary/ © Michael Klinec/Alamy, 22; Photolibrary/ © Jeff Morgan/Alamy, 16; ©
Katrina Brown/Shutterstock, 8 © Elena Elisseeva/Shutterstock, 6 (top), 21.

While every care has been taken to trace and acknowledge copyright, the publisher tenders their
apologies for any accidental infringement where copyright has proved untraceable. Where the attempt
has been unsuccessful, the publisher welcomes information that would redress the situation.

Please note
At the time of printing, the Internet addresses appearing in this book were correct. Owing to the dynamic
nature of the Internet, however, we cannot guarantee that all these addresses will remain correct.

Contents

Glossary words
When a word is printed in **bold**, you can look up its meaning in the Glossary on page 31.

Facing global issues

Hi there! This is Earth speaking. Will you spare a moment to listen to me? I have some very important things to discuss.

We must face up to some urgent environmental problems! All living things depend on my environment, but the way you humans are living at the moment, I will not be able to keep looking after you.

The issues I am worried about are:
- the effects of **global warming**
- the health of natural environments
- the use of **non-renewable** energy supplies
- the environmental impact of unsustainable cities
- the build-up of toxic waste in the environment
- a reliable water supply for all.

My global challenge to you is to find a sustainable way of living. Read on to find out what people around the world are doing to try to help.

Fast fact
Sustainable development is a form of growth that lets us meet our present needs while leaving resources for future generations to meet their needs too.

What's the issue?
Developing renewable energy

Today, supplies of fossil fuels such as oil, gas and coal are running low. **Fossil fuels** are a non-renewable resource that will soon be used up. People need to develop clean, **renewable** energy supplies that will not run out.

Problems with fossil fuels

Supplies of fossil fuels, such as coal, are declining across the world. Coal is a non-renewable resource that is used to **generate** most of the world's electricity. Oil is another non-renewable resource, and it is used as fuel for transport. When these fossil fuels are burnt, a type of **greenhouse gas** called carbon dioxide is produced. Carbon dioxide is adding to global warming.

The need for renewable energy

As Earth's population grows, more energy will need to be produced. Renewable energy is energy that comes from sources that cannot be used up, such as the wind or the Sun. Sources of renewable energy, such as wind power and **solar power**, need to be developed into reliable power supplies.

> **Fast fact**
> In 2007, only 0.8 per cent of electricity in the United States was generated from renewable sources.

Coal is a fossil fuel used to generate electricity for many homes, offices and schools.

Renewable energy issues

Around the globe, issues with renewable energy supplies include:
- too little energy generated from renewable sources (see issue 1)
- the high costs of switching to renewable energy sources (see issue 2)
- difficulties with making renewable energy supplies reliable (see issue 3)
- problems with developing renewable transport fuels (see issue 4)
- making renewable energy sustainable (see issue 5).

ARCTIC OCEAN

Arctic Circle

NORTH
AMERICA
United States

NORTH
ATLANTI
OCEAN

Brazil
SOUTH
AMERICA

ISSUE 4

United States
Biofuel crops, grown to replace fossil fuels, are causing environmental problems. See pages 20–23.

Fast fact
Some countries are exploring a process called **carbon sequestration** to find out if coal can be made into a non-polluting source of power.

ISSUE 5

Brazil
Land is being cleared to grow biofuels for transport. See pages 24–27.

around the globe

ISSUE 3

Finland
Depends on fossil fuels to make its energy supplies reliable. See pages 16–19.

Finland

EUROPE

ASIA

China

Japan

NORTH

PACIFIC

Tropic of Cancer

OCEAN

AFRICA

INDIAN

OCEAN

Equator

ISSUE 1

China
Most energy is generated from non-renewable sources. See pages 8–11.

ISSUE 2

Japan
Nuclear incidents have caused damage to the environment. See pages 12–15.

Too little renewable energy

Most of the energy in **industrial societies** comes from non-renewable fossil fuels. Burning fossil fuels to produce energy releases harmful greenhouse gases, which contribute to global warming. Progress towards replacing fossil fuels with clean, renewable sources of energy has been slow. Not enough support has gone into developing alternatives.

Sources of energy

Energy can come from renewable or non-renewable sources. Fossil fuels such as oil, coal, natural gas and **nuclear power** are non-renewable. There are only limited amounts of these resources. Solar power, wind power and wave power are renewable. They are generated every time the wind blows or the Sun shines.

Non-renewable and renewable energy sources	
Non-renewable energy sources	**Renewable energy sources**
oil	solar power
coal	wind power
natural gas	wave power
nuclear power	**geothermal** power
	biofuels
	hydroelectricity

Replacing fossil fuels

It has been known for decades that non-renewable fossil fuels will run out and must be replaced. However, fossil fuels are still the main sources of energy in most countries. Although clean, alternative sources of energy are available, they need to be developed urgently, to minimise damage to the environment and keep energy supplies from running out.

Most vehicles still run on fossil fuels, such as petrol and diesel.

China is the world's largest coal producer, but it still imports coal to meet its high energy demands.

CASE STUDY
Non-renewable energy in China

ISSUE 1

China has the fastest growing economy in the world. In 2007, China overtook the United States as the world's biggest producer of greenhouse gases.

Energy use in China

Most of China's energy comes from non-renewable sources, and this is likely to continue in the future. In 2003 about two-thirds of China's energy came from burning coal, and almost no energy came from renewable sources. In 2005 the National People's Congress passed a law to increase the use of renewable energy to 15 per cent by 2020. However, most of China's energy will still be produced by burning coal.

Growth of coal use

The use of coal in China is growing, despite the government's laws to increase the use of renewable energy. Coal is still China's cheapest source of energy, and many companies do not want to pay more for energy from renewable sources. In 2006, two new coal-fired power stations were built in China every week. Many of these new power stations release large amounts of pollution.

Fast fact
Some coal-fired power stations produce sulphur dioxide, the chemical that produces **acid rain**, and the greenhouse gas carbon dioxide.

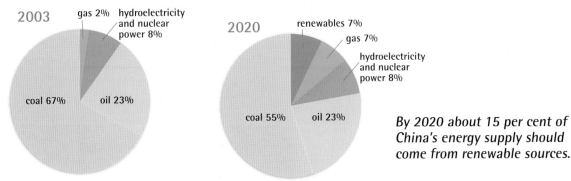

2003
gas 2%
hydroelectricity and nuclear power 8%
coal 67%
oil 23%

2020
renewables 7%
gas 7%
hydroelectricity and nuclear power 8%
coal 55%
oil 23%

By 2020 about 15 per cent of China's energy supply should come from renewable sources.

Towards a sustainable future: Developing new technologies

Developing new technologies can allow people to produce energy from a range of renewable sources.

Types of new technologies

Many different types of new technologies are being developed to make renewable energy more reliable and easier to produce. These technologies include:

- solar panels, **photovoltaic panels** and **concentrated solar power** (CSP)
- wind-turbine farms
- waste-to-energy power generation
- geothermal power stations
- wave power.

Combining new technologies

No single source of renewable energy can replace fossil fuels, but combining a range of new technologies to produce renewable energy can help. Different technologies can be used in different locations, and for different purposes.

Scientists are developing new technologies to generate solar power.

Each Pelamis unit in Portugal's Aguçadoura wave farm is about the size of a commuter train.

CASE STUDY
Wave power in Portugal

In 2007, the world's first commercial wave-power farm was established. It is located five kilometres off the Atlantic coast of Portugal, near Aguçadoura.

The Aguçadoura wave farm

The Aguçadoura wave farm is the world's first multi-unit wave farm. It also is the first commercial wave farm to use wave energy converter technology. The farm uses a set of worm-like collectors called Pelamis units. Pelamis units, which were named after the Latin word for sea snake, were developed in Scotland.

It has been estimated that the wave farm will generate enough electricity to supply more than 1500 Portuguese households and save more than 6000 tonnes of carbon emissions each year.

Advantages and disadvantages of wave power	
Advantages	**Disadvantages**
Can produce large amounts of energy	Produces variable amounts of energy, depending on the strength of the waves
Does not need any fuel to run	Needs to be located in areas with powerful and consistent waves
Does not produce any waste	Must be able to withstand very rough weather
Does not cost much to operate	Can be noisy

Costs of renewable energy

Many sources of renewable energy can be expensive. They may also impact on people and the environment.

Financial costs

Investing in technology to create renewable energy can be expensive. Many countries produce little or no renewable energy because the financial costs are too high. It is expensive to build a hydroelectric power station or a wave farm, and even the cost of adding solar panels to people's homes can add up.

Social and environmental costs

Switching to renewable energy also has costs for people and the environment. Most industrial societies use coal-fired power plants to generate electricity, and oil to run cars, ships and planes. New power plants and systems need to be built to make use of renewable energy. New engines need to be designed for cars, ships and planes to run on fuel from renewable energy sources. Some alternatives to fossil fuels also have the potential to cause damage to the environment. Accidents at nuclear power plants can have devastating consequences for natural ecosystems and human populations.

Building dams and hydroelectricity plants can cause damage to the environment.

Fast fact
In the future, research may show that there are no completely 'clean' ways to use coal or oil.

The Kashiwasaki nuclear power plant in Japan is the largest nuclear power plant in the world.

CASE STUDY
The Kashiwasaki incident

On 16 July 2007, an earthquake shook the Kashiwasaki nuclear power plant in Japan. The incident showed that Japan's nuclear power plants may not be earthquake-proof.

The Kashiwasaki incident

The earthquake at Kashiwasaki measured 6.8 on the Richter Scale, and caused a significant amount of damage. Equipment caught fire, barrels fell and 1300 litres of **radioactive coolant** leaked into the Sea of Japan.

Potential for future incidents

Following the Kashiwasaki incident, some people have been concerned that more serious nuclear incidents could happen if a major earthquake occurs in Japan. Nuclear power plants use dangerous **radioactive material** to generate energy. Japan has over 56 nuclear power plants, and many of them are located in areas prone to earthquakes.

Towards a sustainable future: Reducing environmental costs

The environmental costs of renewable energy can be reduced if people choose technologies with few environmental impacts. Many of the technologies used to produce solar power have few environmental impacts.

Choosing the right sources

The best sources of renewable energy must:
- cause little environmental damage
- be renewable, so that they will not run out
- give a reliable supply of energy when it is needed.

Solar power technologies

Some technologies used to produce solar power have few environmental costs.
- Sunlight on mirrors: large numbers of mirrors can be placed in fields and deserts to concentrate the Sun's energy to generate large amounts of electricity.
- Solar panels: panels can be placed on the roofs of homes and offices to generate small amounts of electricity.
- Passive solar technology: heat from the Sun can be used to warm homes and offices naturally, reducing the need for energy to power heaters.

Fast fact
In 2007, China invested 10 billion dollars on renewable energy. This is double the amount that the United States spent on renewable energy in 2006.

Solar panels on roofs can generate solar power to be used in homes.

The Blue Lagoon, a popular tourist site in Iceland, is heated by natural geothermal power.

CASE STUDY

Geothermal power in Iceland

Geothermal power is generated from heat in **molten rock** under the Earth's surface. Today, geothermal power is being used to provide electricity in Iceland.

How geothermal power works

Heat from molten rocks under the ground can be used as geothermal power. Earth's crust exerts pressure on molten rock to keep it heated. The Sun also warms rock during the day. Some geothermal power is released naturally through volcanoes, hot springs and geysers. The Blue Lagoon in Iceland is a natural hot spring.

Iceland's supply of geothermal power

Iceland's supply of geothermal power provides electricity to many towns. Today in Iceland, whole towns are heated using geothermal energy. About 85 per cent of all homes in Iceland are heated using hot spring water.

Iceland is the only **developed country** to generate all its energy from renewable sources. Hydroelectricity stations produce 83 per cent of Iceland's electricity, and geothermal power stations produce the other 17 per cent.

Fast fact

Early civilisations used geothermal power to cook, fire pottery and heat spas. Over 2000 years ago, Roman villas had floors heated by natural hot springs.

Making renewable energy reliable

Many sources of renewable energy are unreliable because they depend on changeable elements in the environment, such as water, sunlight and wind.

Unreliable supplies of wind power

Wind power is an unreliable source of renewable energy, because wind turbines only generate energy when the wind blows. If the weather is calm, wind turbines will not turn, and no energy will be generated. If the weather is too stormy, wind turbines may produce more energy than can be captured. Therefore, much of the energy generated in very windy periods may be lost. Wind power is often only used to supplement reliable forms of power, such as nuclear energy or coal-fired power.

Unreliable supplies of solar power

Solar power can be another unreliable source of renewable energy, as solar panels only collect sunlight when the Sun is shining. If the weather is cloudy, solar systems may need to be boosted by energy from other sources, or by a backup battery.

Power stored in batteries can be used to back up solar systems when there is no sunlight, such as at night or on cloudy days.

Fast fact
In the past, it has proved difficult to create large, reliable battery systems to store power from renewable energy sources such as wind power and solar power.

Many workers still work in Finland's coal-fired power stations, which generate much of Finland's electricity.

CASE STUDY

Unreliable energy supplies in Finland

Finland is a cold country that needs large amounts of energy to heat homes and offices. While Finland uses energy from renewable sources, it still depends on energy from non-renewable sources because they are reliable.

Using fossil fuels

Finland brings in fossil fuels from other countries to supplement its energy supply. Burning fossil fuels releases greenhouse gas emissions and contributes to global warming. Many people in Finland would like to see more energy come from clean, renewable sources, such as hydroelectricity, wind power and solar power.

Fast fact
Finland is now importing more natural gas and less coal, because natural gas releases less carbon emissions than coal for each unit of energy produced.

Using nuclear power

Finland also uses nuclear power to supplement its energy supply. Finland currently has four nuclear power plants, and it has been suggested that a fifth may be built. Today, there is less opposition to nuclear power in Finland than there once was, as the population is becoming more aware of the need to reduce the country's dependence on fossil fuels.

Towards a sustainable future: Storing excess energy

Many types of batteries and storage systems can store excess energy for later use. This makes many sources of renewable energy more reliable.

More reliable energy supplies

Batteries and storage systems can store electricity and make electricity supplies more reliable. Electricity demand is uneven, as more electricity is used at certain times of the day or at different times of the year. When it is very hot or cold, large amounts of electricity are used for heating or cooling. These times are called peak periods. Periods when little electricity is used are called off-peak periods. In off-peak periods, energy could be stored in order to create a reliable supply for peak periods.

Fast fact
Geothermal power is a reliable source of energy. Heat from rocks is always available beneath Earth's surface.

Different types of storage

There are many different types of batteries and storage systems available. Some of these technologies are listed in the table below.

Name of storage technology	How it works
pumped hydro-storage	pumps water into hydroelectricity storage dams
flow batteries	huge tanks of chemicals store electricity as chemical energy
magnetic energy storage	coils held at very low temperatures store high-energy magnetic fields
hydrogen storage	water is split into hydrogen and oxygen, and the hydrogen is burnt when electricity is needed

Wind power is stored in underground air chambers at the Iowa Stored Energy Park.

CASE STUDY

Iowa Stored Energy Park

Iowa Stored Energy Park in the United States is creating an energy storage system for its large wind power station. During peak periods, wind can be released and used in power stations.

Making wind energy reliable

At Iowa Stored Energy Park, wind energy can be stored to provide a reliable electricity supply on demand. The park will be environmentally friendly and cost-efficient. It has been designed to use some of the latest technologies, such as:

- modern wind turbines
- air combustion turbines
- underground air batteries.

Underground air batteries

Iowa has many underground chambers that can be used to store **compressed air**. These underground chambers can be used to create an 'underground air battery' to store excess wind energy generated in Iowa.

Fast fact
In Utah, windmills were once used to pump water from beneath the ground. Extra water was stored to use at a later time, when the wind would not blow.

Renewable transport fuels

There are few reliable sources of renewable energy that can be used as transport fuels. Biofuels, or fuel made from plants, are one reliable alternative to fossil fuels, but they have many negative environmental impacts.

Lack of renewable fuels

It is proving difficult to develop renewable fuels to power cars, aeroplanes and ships. Many of the fuels used to power cars are not sustainable in the long term. There are fewer alternative fuels available for aeroplanes and ships than there are for cars and trucks. In some places, hydrogen fuel is being trialled as an alternative fuel. However, it is very expensive to produce.

Biofuels

Biofuels are renewable energy sources that are often used to replace fossil fuels.

- Corn and rapeseed are used to replace or supplement oil.
- Corn and sugarcane crops are used to make bio-ethanol, which can replace gasoline.
- Rape seed and palm oil are turned into bio-diesel, which can be used instead of diesel.

However, biofuels have many negative environmental impacts. Biofuel crops need large amounts of land and water to grow, and these resources are needed to grow food crops.

Sugarcane is used to make bio-ethanol, which can be used to run cars.

Fast fact
The Intergovernmental Panel on Climate Change (IPCC) estimates that two per cent of global carbon emissions come from aeroplanes.

Corn is used to make ethanol, a biofuel used in transport.

CASE STUDY
Biofuels in the United States

Biofuel crops in the United States are having negative impacts on the environment.

Environmental impacts of biofuels

Planting and growing biofuels have many negative impacts on the environment.
* Biofuel crops take up large areas of land that is needed for food crops.
* Biofuel crops use large amounts of water that is needed to irrigate food crops and supply local communities.
* Fertilisers used on biofuels often release greenhouse gases and contribute to global warming.

Not enough biofuels

The number of biofuel crops in the United States is increasing, but there is still not enough to meet demand. In 2007, the United States announced a strategy to reduce oil use in transport by 20 per cent by 2017. The key idea to achieve this was to increase the use of biofuels. It has been calculated that the amount of corn needed to meet the United States' biofuel targets is greater than the total amount of corn currently grown in the country.

Fast fact
In 2008 about one per cent of Earth's crops were grown to be used as biofuels.

Towards a sustainable future: Developing renewable fuels

New sources of renewable transport fuels are being explored to find replacements for fossil fuels. These new sources of fuel are also being used more efficiently.

New sources of renewable fuel

New sources of renewable fuel are being developed as demand for fuels increases and oil supplies decline. These sources of energy are being used to power many forms of transport, including:

- hydrogen-powered trains
- solar-powered cars
- electric cars.

Efficient use of fuel

The **consumption** of non-renewable and renewable fuels is being decreased as people use fuel more efficiently. Aeroplanes and cars with more fuel-efficient engines can move people greater distances while using less fuel.

Fast fact

Today, many airlines are trialling the use of hydrogen fuel. Hydrogen fuel may have negative environmental impacts, such as causing noise pollution.

Hydrogen fuel cells are being used to run public buses in Berlin, Germany.

Hydrogen-powered trains are powered by hydrogen batteries.

CASE STUDY
Hydrogen-powered trains

Hydrogen-powered trains are energy-efficient and better for the environment than diesel and some electric trains. In 2007, the world's first hydrogen-powered passenger train ran through Japan's Yatsugatake Mountains.

Hydrogen fuel cells

Hydrogen-powered trains run on hydrogen fuel cells, so they do not need power lines like electric trains. Hydrogen from the fuel cells combines with oxygen from the air to supply energy. The only waste from this process is water. The United Kingdom Rail Safety and Standards Board claims that using hydrogen instead of diesel could cut greenhouse gas emissions by at least one quarter.

Producing hydrogen

Scientists are developing methods to produce hydrogen cheaply and efficiently. Today, most hydrogen is produced using natural gas and steam. In the future, technology may be available to produce hydrogen by photosynthesis, a process used to capture energy from the Sun. Algae and bacteria could be used to store the energy of sunlight as hydrogen.

Fast fact
Canada plans to build a hydrogen-powered passenger train in time for the 2010 Winter Olympics.

Unsustainable renewable energy

Not all sources of renewable energy are sustainable. Some sources have negative impacts on the environment, while others will become unsustainable if they are not supplemented with other sources.

Impacts on the environment

Many sources of renewable energy are not sustainable because they have negative impacts on the environment. Biofuels take large amounts of land and water to grow. Dams that are built to hold water for hydroelectricity may cause damage to local fish populations.

Making sources of energy unsustainable

Some sources of renewable energy will become unsustainable unless they are supplemented with other sources. Most sources of renewable energy cannot provide a sustainable energy supply in all locations. Biofuels can be used to supplement other energy sources, but they will become unsustainable if they are used as a major source of energy because they use large amounts of land and water to grow.

Concentrated solar power (CSP) is a more sustainable and reliable source of renewable energy than many other sources.

In Brazil, large areas of land are being cleared to grow soybeans.

CASE STUDY

The impacts of growing soybeans in Brazil

In Brazil, large areas of land have been cleared to grow soybeans for biofuels. As rainforest is being cleared, rainfall is decreasing.

Clearing of rainforest

Today about 13 per cent of the Brazilian rainforest has been cleared, and 15 per cent of this cleared area is being used to grow soybeans. As the demand for biofuels grows each year, more land is being cleared to grow soybean crops. The International Institute of Environment and Development in London predicts that more rainforest will be cleared in the future, and food prices will increase as land to grow food crops decreases.

Falling rainfall levels

Rainfall levels are also falling in areas that have been cleared to grow soybeans. These areas are slowly changing from tropical rainforest into drier rainforest. Areas cleared to plant soybean crops have been shown to receive even less rainfall than areas cleared for grazing.

> **Fast fact**
> When the biofuel bio-ethanol is burned, it releases acetaldehyde, which reacts with sunlight to form ozone. Ozone is a key ingredient in air pollution such as smog.

Towards a sustainable future: Making renewable energy sustainable

Many sources of renewable energy can be made sustainable by combining them with other sources. Biofuels can also be made from crops that can be grown sustainably.

Combining energy sources

Combining energy sources is the most likely way to ensure a sustainable energy supply. Today, scientists are searching for ways to combine energy sources. In France, the International Thermonuclear Experimental Reactor project is exploring the use of **nuclear fusion**. In the United States, a range of solar power sources are also being explored, including CSP and space-based solar power collection. It has been estimated that 39 000 square kilometres of CSP in southwest United States could supply half of the country's energy needs.

Sustainable biofuels

New forms of renewable energy, such as sustainable biofuels, are being developed around the world. Sustainable biofuels could include:

- crops that can grow where food plants cannot
- crops that require little or no fresh water to grow
- organic waste or water plants that produce methane or bio-gas
- algae farms and other biomass projects that do not affect food supply.

Fast fact
CSP has been used in the Mohave Desert's Eldorado Valley for 20 years. It supplies electricity to 35 000 people.

Biomass projects, such as algae farms, can contribute to sustainable energy supplies.

The energy from falling rain could be a new source of renewable energy in the future.

CASE STUDY

Energy from falling rain

Researchers in France are exploring the possibility of using the energy from falling raindrops to generate electricity.

Using the push of rain

People standing in heavy rain can feel the pressure of raindrops on their bodies. This is known as the 'push' of rain, and it is one untapped source of renewable energy. We already use the push of running water to generate electricity, but using the push of falling raindrops is a new idea.

Different-sized raindrops give different amounts of push. Rain often falls when the Sun is not shining, so energy from raindrops could be collected at times when solar power is not available.

Developing new technology

Researchers are developing technology to collect raindrops and generate electricity. Some plastic-based materials can convert the push of rain into electricity. These are called **piezoelectric** materials. Raindrops hitting the flexible surface on the piezoelectric material set off vibrations that can produce electricity.

Fast fact
Cold fusion, in which two atoms join together at low temperatures, is still being investigated as a possible source of renewable energy. Many scientists believe that this is not possible.

What can you do?
Use renewable energy

Each person can help to reduce energy use and use more renewable energy. If every person does this, the differences will add up.

Investigate renewable sources

You could investigate how to increase the use of renewable energy in your community by:

- contacting local energy providers to learn which sources of renewable energy are available to your community
- inspecting your community for evidence of renewable energy sources, such as solar hot-water collectors or solar panels on roofs
- interviewing local council members about sources of renewable energy
- researching grants for using renewable energy that your family, school or community may be eligible for.

Fast fact
People in countries across Earth turn off their lights and appliances during Earth Hour, which is held once a year.

Riding your bike to a friend's house instead of being driven is one way to reduce energy use.

Reduce your energy consumption

Even if you do not use energy from renewable sources, you can still reduce the amount of energy you consume. Each day, try to perform one action that could reduce your energy consumption. These actions could include:

- switching off electrical appliances when they are not needed
- asking your family or teachers to use energy-efficient lights
- opening and closing curtains and windows to control the temperature in your home naturally
- walking or riding a bike on short trips, rather than travelling by car
- putting on more clothes to keep warm, rather than turning on a heater.

Using energy-efficient lights in your home is one way to reduce energy consumption.

Well, I hope you now see that if you take up my challenge your world will be a better place. There are many ways to work towards a sustainable future. Imagine it... a world with:

- decreasing rates of global warming
- protected ecosystems for all living things
- renewable fuel for most forms of transport
- sustainable city development
- low risks of exposure to toxic substances
- a safe and reliable water supply for all.

This is what you can achieve if you work together with my natural systems.

We must work together to live sustainably. That will mean a better environment and a better life for all living things on Earth, now and in the future.

Websites

For further information on renewable energy, visit these websites:
- National Renewable Energy Council www.nrel.gov/learning/
- Energy Information Administration (EIA)
  www.eia.doe.gov/kids/energyfacts/sources/renewable/renewable.html
- ITER fusion project www.iter.org/index.htm

Glossary

acid rain
polluted rain that contains dangerous chemicals

biofuel
fuel made from living materials, such as plants

carbon sequestration
burying carbon wastes from coal-fired power stations deep under ground, so they do not pollute the atmosphere

compressed air
air held under pressure

concentrated solar power
a technology that uses large mirrors to concentrate the Sun's rays into chambers full of oil, where it is heated to make electricity

consumption
amount of materials used

developed country
a country with industrial development, a strong economy and a high standard of living

fossil fuels
fuels such as oil, coal and gas, which formed under Earth millions of years ago

generate
make or produce

geothermal
heat from inside Earth

global warming
a rise in average temperatures on Earth

greenhouse gas
a gas that helps to trap the Sun's heat in the atmosphere

industrial societies
societies with large industries that use lots of energy

molten rock
hot rock that has been changed to liquid form

non-renewable
a resource that is limited in supply and cannot be replaced once it runs out

nuclear fusion
a chemical reaction that combines small atoms into larger ones by releasing energy

nuclear power
a source of energy produced by nuclear fusion

photovoltaic panels
panels that convert light into electricity

piezoelectric
plastic-based materials that create electricity

radioactive material
material that gives off radiation, which can cause sickness in living things

radioactive coolant
a substance used to cool hot radioactive materials

renewable
a resource with a constant supply, so it cannot run out

solar power
energy that is generated from the Sun's rays

Index